Unicorns Don't Give Sleigh Rides

by **Debbie Dadey**
and
Marcia Thornton Jones

illustrated by **John Steven Gurney**

A
LITTLE APPLE
PAPERBACK

SCHOLASTIC INC.
New York   Toronto   London   Auckland   Sydney

No part of this publication may be reproduced in whole or in part, or stored in a retrieval system, or transmitted in any form or by any means, electronic, mechanical, photocopying, recording, or otherwise, without written permission of the publisher. For information regarding permission, write to Scholastic Inc., Attention: Permissions Department, 555 Broadway, New York, NY 10012.

ISBN 0-590-25783-8

Text copyright © 1997 by Marcia Thornton Jones and Debra S. Dadey.
Illustrations copyright © 1997 by Scholastic Inc.
All rights reserved. Published by Scholastic Inc.
LITTLE APPLE PAPERBACKS is a trademark of Scholastic Inc.
THE ADVENTURES OF THE BAILEY SCHOOL KIDS in design is a registered trademark of Scholastic Inc.

12   0 1/0 2/0

Printed in the U.S.A.   40

First Scholastic printing, November 1997

Book design by Laurie Williams

Dedicated to Krystal, Pistol Pete, Jessie, Muffles, Bailey, Cleo, and all the lovable animals waiting in shelters — and to people dedicated to finding homes for furry friends!

— DD and MTJ

Contents

1

Whole Truth

"Are you sure you can make it?" Melody asked Liza.

Liza pushed her blond bangs out of her eyes and nodded. "It only hurts a little."

Liza and Melody and their two friends, Howie and Eddie, were making their way down the long road to the Bailey City Stables. They had to walk slowly because Liza limped with every step.

Usually the four friends would be in school, but so much snow fell the night before that school was canceled. Even though it was too cold for Liza's riding lesson, she still had to take care of her pony, Penelope. Melody, Howie, and Eddie had promised to help with her stable duties before playing in the snow.

Eddie pulled his baseball cap down over his curly red hair. "If you weren't such a klutz, you wouldn't have fallen down," he said.

"Liza's not clumsy," Melody said. "She probably slipped on all this snow."

"Exactly what *did* happen to your ankle?" Howie asked.

Liza took a deep breath. "It was the strangest thing," she said.

"There's nothing strange about you falling down," Eddie laughed. "You aren't exactly the world's best athlete."

Melody punched Eddie on the arm. "Be nice," Melody warned.

"Falling down wasn't strange," Liza said after giving Eddie the meanest look she could. "It's what happened after I fell."

"Go on," Howie said to Liza. "Tell us what happened."

"I was brushing Penelope. That's the pony I've been taking care of since I started taking riding lessons. I brushed her extra long because I want her coat to be shiny when she gives sleigh rides at the mall. By the time I finished, everyone else was gone except Mr. Withers, the owner of the Bailey City Stables. I went out the side door and slipped on the ice."

"That must have really hurt," Melody said.

Liza nodded. "It hurt so badly I couldn't walk. Mr. Withers didn't know I was out there, and it was cold. I thought I would turn into a giant icicle!"

Eddie laughed. "That wouldn't be so bad. At least icicles don't have to go to school!"

Howie ignored Eddie. "How did you make it back to the stable?" he asked.

"I was getting ready to yell for help when I heard them . . . jingle bells coming closer and closer," Liza said. "A sleigh came through the swirling snow pulled by a pearl-colored horse. The horse stopped right beside me. I dragged myself inside the empty sleigh and that horse went right to the stable as if it knew exactly what to do."

Melody nodded. "It wanted to get out of the snow, too."

"You were lucky," Howie said. "But that's not so strange. They say horses always head back to the stable."

Liza shook her head. "It wasn't luck," she said.

"Then what was it?" Eddie asked.

Liza stopped hobbling. "Do you promise not to laugh," she asked, "if I tell you the truth? The whole truth?"

Melody and Howie nodded. "We promise not to laugh," they both said.

But Eddie shrugged. "I never make promises I can't keep," he said.

"Since when?" Howie asked.

Melody ignored Eddie and Howie and looked at Liza. "Go ahead," Melody said. "Tell us."

Liza looked each of her friends in the

eyes. "That was not a normal horse," she told them. "It had a horn between its ears. And you know what that means."

Eddie snorted. "That's easy," he said. "It means you're crazy. But we already knew that."

Liza put her hands on her hips. "It means," Liza said, "that horse isn't a horse at all. It's a unicorn!"

2

Sleigh Rides

Eddie laughed and kicked the snow. "And I'm Pinocchio playing with matches."

Liza's face grew red. "I'm not kidding. It really was a unicorn."

"I'm not kidding, either," Eddie said. "If you think you saw a unicorn yesterday, then you have snow between your ears."

Melody patted Liza's arm. "It was dark out. You probably only *thought* you saw a unicorn."

"I know more about horses than any of you," Liza said. "Even if my ankle was hurting, I can still tell a horse from a unicorn."

"That's easy to do," Howie said, "because there are no such things as unicorns. They're just made-up creatures."

"Then why are there so many books about them in the library?" Liza asked.

"There are books about goblins, too," Eddie said, "and you don't see them hanging around every street corner."

"Have I ever lied to you before?" Liza asked her friends.

"Well, no," Melody admitted. Liza never told lies, not even little white ones.

"We're not saying you lied," Howie said. "We're saying you made a mistake."

"Everybody makes mistakes," Eddie said. "Even me."

"You make lots of them," Liza told Eddie. "But I didn't make a mistake."

Liza was ready to argue more, but just then Howie pointed and said, "Look at that!"

Two shiny black horses trotted down the lane pulling a large green sleigh with gold decorations all over it.

"King Midas would have loved that sleigh," Howie said.

"Forget King Midas," Melody told him. "*I* love the sleigh. I want a ride in it!"

"It costs money," Liza told her. "That's one of the sleighs Mr. Withers is using to give rides at the mall so he can earn money for the stables. The rest he's giving to charity."

"I'm a charity," Eddie told her. He held out his hand. "Please donate to the GEAR fund."

"What in the world is the GEAR fund?" Howie asked.

Eddie smiled. "It's the Give Eddie A Ride fund."

Melody grabbed Eddie's baseball cap and started to bop him with it when the sleigh pulled to a stop right beside them. The short, white-haired man driving the sleigh gave them a big toothy grin. He wore an old-fashioned cap with flaps over his ears, and his nose was red from the cold.

"Hello, Mr. Withers," Liza said politely.

"These are my friends. They came to help me."

"It's always nice to have a few extra hands," Mr. Withers said. "Hop aboard and I'll give you a ride up to the stables."

"Yee-haw!" Eddie yelled as the sleigh glided over the glistening snow.

Liza's eyes sparkled. "This is so magical."

"And real," Eddie said. "Not like your stupid make-believe unicorn."

Suddenly, the sleigh stopped and Mr. Withers looked at Eddie. "Did you say unicorn?" Mr. Withers asked in a deep voice.

Something about the way Mr. Withers looked at him made Eddie lie. "Uh, no," Eddie stammered. "I said popcorn. I like to eat popcorn."

Mr. Withers stared hard at the kids, then he turned around and clucked for the horses to start up again. The kids were silent until Mr. Withers stopped in front of the stable.

"Thank you for the ride," Melody said as the kids jumped out of the sleigh.

Mr. Withers nodded and clucked for the horses to move again.

When Liza got close to the stable door she stopped suddenly. "Oh, my gosh," she cried.

"Is your ankle hurting worse?" Melody asked.

Liza shook her head and gulped. Without a word, she pointed to the side of the stable. Melody, Howie, and Eddie looked. What they saw made them gasp.

3

Winter Wonderland

"It's beautiful," Melody whispered.

Howie nodded. "It looks like a winter wonderland. I've never seen so many poinsettias in one place in my whole life."

The four friends followed the row of plants with big red leaves that started at one corner of the stable and wrapped around the side.

"If you ask me," Eddie said, "it looks like a florist went berserk and tossed flowers everywhere. Either that, or a flower truck slid off the road."

"I don't see any trucks in the ditch," Melody said. All she saw was snow, more snow, and lots of bright red leaves. "I'll bet Mr. Withers is decorating his stable for Christmas."

"Mr. Withers doesn't have time to decorate," Liza pointed out.

"He's too busy giving sleigh rides," Howie added.

"I think he's too weird to put up decorations," Eddie said. "I thought he was going to knock me out of the sleigh when I said *unicorn*."

Howie nodded. "It's almost like he had something to hide."

"Well, he didn't hide these plants," Melody said. "They're beautiful!"

"But why would Mr. Withers put them on the side of his stable?" Howie asked. "Most people decorate the fronts of buildings."

"Mr. Withers didn't put them there," Liza said quietly. "They're growing there, right in the spot where I fell."

Howie pulled his jacket tight around his body. "Don't be silly. It's freezing. Flowers can't grow in this kind of weather. Especially poinsettias. They need lots of warmth."

Liza kneeled down beside one of the bright red blooms. "No one planted these," she said.

"Then how did they grow?" Melody asked. "They didn't just pop up by themselves."

"Yes, they did." Liza stood up carefully on her sore ankle. "There is a legend about unicorns."

Eddie rolled his eyes. "Oh, brother," he said. "Not that kooky talk again."

"It's not kooky," Liza said. "The legend says that wherever a unicorn walks, magical flowers appear."

Melody touched one of the bloodred leaves. "They really do look magical."

Howie shook his head. "These flowers may be pretty, but I'm sure someone put them there. Someone who wanted to spread a little holiday cheer."

"That someone," Liza said, "was a unicorn."

Eddie laughed so hard he fell down in the snow. "The only thing a unicorn planted was silly ideas in your brain," he gasped.

"Don't laugh at Liza," Melody said. "You'll hurt her feelings."

Eddie grabbed a handful of snow and threw it up in the air. "I won't hurt her feelings if she'll stop being so silly."

"Eddie's right," Howie said and tried not to laugh. "You were just seeing things."

"I know what I saw," Liza said. "And I saw a horn. A real unicorn's horn!"

4

Damsel in Distress

Melody patted Liza on the back and nodded. "That's what you think you saw. But with the snow swirling and your ankle hurting so badly, you probably just imagined it."

"Besides," Howie said, "why would a unicorn show up at the Bailey City Stables just to give you a sleigh ride?"

"That's easy," Liza said. "I was a damsel in distress."

"A WHAT!" Eddie yelled. Then he broke into another fit of giggles. Even Melody and Howie laughed out loud.

Liza tried to ignore them, but her face turned bright red. "Everybody knows a unicorn's horn is magic," she snapped. "Unicorns use their horns to help weak things. Especially damsels in distress!"

"That's the silliest thing I've ever heard." Eddie laughed.

Melody and Howie nodded. "You have to admit," Howie said with a giggle, "you don't fit the description of a damsel in distress."

"But my ankle was hurt," Liza blurted. "I needed help. That's why the unicorn came here."

Eddie grabbed a handful of snow and jumped up. "I think we need to knock some sense into Liza. I know just how to do it." Eddie tossed his snowball high in the air. Liza ducked just in time and Eddie's snowball whizzed over her head.

"I'm warning you," Liza told Eddie. "Stop it."

Eddie laughed even harder. "You're such a weakling, you couldn't get a carrot away from a bunny rabbit," he joked. "So I know you can't keep me from bombarding you with snowballs."

Liza shook her head. "I wouldn't want to take a carrot away from a cute bunny," she said. "But there's nothing cute about you. I want you to stop making fun of me."

"And I want you to stop telling fairy tales," Eddie said. Then he threw another snowball.

This time, Liza didn't move fast enough. The snowball hit her on the shoulder.

"You better stop this minute," Liza warned, bending down to scoop up snow. Then she sailed a snowball through the air. Her friends gasped. Especially Eddie, because Liza's snowball hit him hard, right in the middle of his stomach. Eddie grunted and fell back in the snow. He sat on the ground, trying to catch his breath.

Howie and Melody clapped and cheered. "Hooray for Liza!" Melody yelled.

"Who taught you to throw a snowball like that?" Howie asked.

Liza wiped the snow off her mittens and shrugged. "I told you," she said.

"Last night I was a damsel in distress, but today you better watch out because I'm not a weakling anymore! Thanks to the Bailey City unicorn." Then Liza turned and limped into the barn.

Melody and Howie looked at Eddie and laughed. "I guess you won't pick on Liza anymore," Howie said with a smile.

Eddie stood up and wiped off the seat of his pants. "That was just a lucky throw," he said.

Melody laughed even harder. "Lucky for you that it didn't knock you all the way to the North Pole," she said.

"It's not that funny," Eddie snapped, his face turning redder and redder. Howie and Melody followed Liza, but when they opened the stable door Eddie didn't follow them.

"Aren't you coming?" Melody asked.

Eddie shrugged. "If Liza's so strong, she doesn't need my help," he said.

And then Eddie disappeared around the corner of the stable.

5

Magic

More snow started to fall, and Eddie muttered under his breath. Eddie hated to be made fun of, especially by Liza. He was trying to think of some way to get her back. That's why he didn't see it right away.

A huge horse the color of falling snow stood behind the stable. The horse stared straight at Eddie before turning to walk though a small cluster of trees. With every step the horse took, Eddie heard the faint sound of jingle bells.

Eddie followed the white horse, squinting through the swirling snow to get a better look. Every once in a while the horse looked around as if to make sure Eddie was still following.

The horse led Eddie to the far corner

of a field. Then the horse disappeared behind an old barn. Eddie kicked through the snow until he reached the barn. A broken wagon and rusty plows stood beside the barn.

Eddie looked all around, but he didn't see the horse anywhere. He was getting ready to head back to the stable when he heard something. At first, he thought he was hearing the winter wind blowing through the leafless trees. Then he realized it was a tiny whine coming from inside the barn.

Eddie opened the door and blinked to get used to the darkness inside. That's when he saw a tiny gray-and-white kitten huddled in the corner. The kitten was trembling.

When Eddie scooped up the kitten, she tried to crawl inside his coat.

"You shouldn't be out here in the cold," Eddie told her. "I'll take you where it's warm."

Eddie closed the barn door and

trudged back to the stable as fast as he could. As soon as Melody, Liza, and Howie saw him they knew something was wrong.

Eddie bent down and dumped the kitten in the middle of some straw. "Look what I found in an old barn," he said.

Liza cradled the kitten next to her cheek. "That's odd," she said. "Nobody uses that old barn. What were you doing out there?"

Eddie grinned. "Following a huge white horse. If it wasn't for the horse, I wouldn't have found this little curtain clinger," Eddie said, pointing to the kitten. "You should learn to ride that horse instead of your nag, Penelope."

Liza hugged the kitten and shook her head. "No one can ride magic," she said in a quiet voice.

"That's a good name for a horse," Eddie said.

"Magic isn't his name," Liza said. "Magic is what he is. And this kitten proves it! That horse was really a unicorn leading you right to this kitten!"

Eddie stared at Liza for a minute, then he laughed. "I didn't get to see the horse up close, but I know it was definitely not a unicorn," he said. Then Eddie reached out and pulled the kitten's tail.

The kitten turned and bopped Eddie on the hand with her claw. Melody and Howie laughed. Eddie jerked his hand away to make sure he wasn't bleeding.

"That kitten sure acts like a normal cat," Howie said.

"Just like that horse was an ordinary horse," Eddie said. "He was even wearing one of Mr. Withers' jingle bells."

"Eddie must be right," Melody said. "After all, unicorns don't live in Bailey City."

"And they definitely don't give third-graders sleigh rides," Howie added.

Eddie nodded. "That horse I saw was just a horse," he said. "And I have a plan to prove it!"

6

Happy Trails

"Mom says I can keep the kitten if no one claims it," Liza said on Saturday. Mr. Withers had harnessed Penelope to a giant sleigh, and Liza was taking the kids for a ride down the lane. "I'm going to name my kitten Jingle Bells," Liza told her friends.

"*Dumbbells* would be a better name," Eddie teased.

Liza started to make a face at Eddie, but Melody stopped her. "Speaking of bells," Melody told her friends, "listen!" The four kids sat very still in the sleigh. In the distance, behind a stand of trees, came the faint jingle of bells.

"It's the unicorn!" Liza shrieked and shook the reins so Penelope would trot faster.

Liza steered Penelope to an old barn. It was the same barn where Eddie had found the kitten.

"This place looks deserted," Melody said. "We better get back on the lane to the stables."

Liza pointed to a row of new red flowers beside the old barn. "That almost looks like a path to me." Without a word, Liza stepped out of the sleigh and walked toward the deep red flowers.

"Can we go to the stable now?" Eddie asked. "In case you haven't noticed, it's freezing out here."

"Just a minute," Liza told him. "I think these flowers are leading us somewhere."

Eddie rolled his eyes. "I think you're leading me to frostbite city."

Liza and the poinsettias stopped right in front of a wooden door. A shiny new sleigh bell hung on the door, swaying in the cold wind.

"There's your unicorn sound," Howie said, pointing to the bell.

"Hey," Eddie said. "That wasn't there yesterday."

"Shhh," Liza said. "That's not all I hear. It sounds like something crying." Liza pulled open the wooden door and went inside the dark barn. Melody, Howie, and Eddie followed her close behind.

"I'm going to be crying pretty soon," Eddie complained, "if I don't get my nose warm."

"Look," Melody cried, rushing over to a tiny ball of fur in a corner. "It's a baby dog."

"A puppy," Howie corrected her.

"It's a mutt," Eddie corrected them both.

The tiny black-and-white puppy licked Melody on the nose. "It's so sweet," Melody said. "We can't leave her here or she'll freeze."

"I'll take her home until we find her owners," Howie volunteered. "My dad won't mind. He likes dogs."

"Let's take the mutt and go," Eddie

suggested, "before we all turn into frozen corn dogs."

Howie picked up the puppy and led Melody, Eddie, and Liza back out into the bright snow-covered woods. The sleigh bell over the door jingled again when a breeze stirred it.

"I wonder who put that bell there," Melody said.

"It was there so we would find this puppy, and I know who put it there," Liza said. "The unicorn!"

"Even if there was a unicorn," Melody said, "it couldn't reach up and tie a bell above the barn door."

"Not unless," Liza said slowly, "it had help from Mr. Withers!"

"Mr. Withers is a nice guy," Howie agreed. "But I don't think he'd hide a unicorn."

"People would pay to see a unicorn," Melody added. "And he's always trying to earn money for the poor."

"He's always doing good deeds," Liza

said with a nod. "Maybe he didn't open these stables to earn money. Maybe he's here on a mission. A unicorn mission!"

7

Crazy

"Are you starting that crazy unicorn talk again?" Eddie asked. "I was hoping you'd forgotten that nonsense."

Howie put the puppy inside his jacket and looked at Liza. "It's just a lucky coincidence that the bell was hanging on the barn door."

"Lucky might be a good name for Howie's puppy," Melody suggested.

Howie put up one hand. "Wait a minute. I'm only giving her a home until we find a better place."

The puppy stuck its head out of Howie's jacket and licked his chin. Melody, Eddie, and Liza laughed. "I think she likes where she is right now," Liza said as they climbed back into the

sleigh and directed Penelope to pull them back to the stable.

"Bailey," Howie said slowly. "That's a nice name for a dog, too."

"I always liked Spot," Eddie said.

"Maybe I'll look up names tonight," Howie told his friends as Penelope stopped in front of the stable and the kids climbed out of the sleigh.

"Don't tell me you have a book of names," Eddie laughed. He knew Howie liked to read, but he couldn't imagine reading a book full of names.

Howie nodded. "Sure I do. And so do you. In fact, just about everybody does. It's called the phone book!"

"Speaking of looking up things," Liza said, "I looked up unicorns last night. I found out that everything I told you about unicorns is true. Flowers grow where they walk, their horns are magic, and they help weak things in distress."

"You're as distressing as it gets," Eddie joked.

Liza put her hands on her hips. "I'm not just talking about me. I'm talking about this puppy and my kitten, Jingle Bells. The unicorn's magic saved them both."

Eddie picked up some snow and threw it in the air. "You need magic to knock sense into your head. Let's get in that stable and I'll prove, once and for all, there are no such things as unicorns!"

8

The Trap

"Ohhh," Melody moaned. "My ankle hurts!"

"Moan louder," Eddie told her. "You have to sound convincing."

Eddie, Howie, and Liza stood in an empty stall in the stable. The puppy snuggled in a bed of straw. Melody sprawled on the floor, pretending she had hurt her ankle. Liza folded her arms in front of her chest. "This isn't right," Liza said. "You shouldn't try to trick a unicorn."

"It's not a unicorn," Eddie said. "But if your unicorn is real, it will come to help Melody."

"This won't work," Melody said from her seat on the stable floor.

Eddie frowned. "It will work if you

groan loud enough. Come on, let me hear it."

"OHHHHHHH!" Melody screamed.

"That's it," Eddie said. He looked at Howie and Liza and told them, "You two get out of here so my plan will work."

Liza rolled her eyes and pulled Howie's arm. "Come on," Liza said. "You can help me brush Penelope."

For twenty minutes, Liza and Howie brushed Penelope. Eddie hid behind a pile of straw and Melody moaned. She moaned and moaned. "I'm getting a sore throat," Melody finally complained.

"Shhh," Eddie hissed from behind the straw. "Moan some more. Something is coming."

Melody's eyes got wide as the stall door squeaked open. "OHHHHHHH!" she moaned.

Creak. Creeeeak. The door slowly swung open. Eddie got ready to pounce. Melody groaned again and closed her eyes.

"What's going on here?" asked Mr. Withers, the stable owner. "Are you all right?"

Melody's face got red and she jumped up from the floor. "Oh, yes," she said quickly. "I was just playing."

Mr. Withers shook his head. "I thought someone was really hurt. I was about to call for help."

Eddie leaped out from his hiding place as Mr. Withers walked back out the stall door. Howie and Liza came to see what had happened.

Liza giggled as soon as the door closed again. "I told you it wouldn't work."

"And why not?" Eddie said. "It was a perfectly good plan. The unicorn never came, so I proved it isn't real!"

"Your plan had one thing missing," Howie told him. "Remember, Liza told us that unicorns like to rescue *helpless* creatures."

"So what?" Melody asked.

"Melody is anything but helpless," Liza told her friends. "Melody could beat up Eddie if she wanted."

Eddie wanted to argue, but he was afraid Melody would try to prove Liza and Howie were right.

"Your plan didn't work," Howie said. "But you were on the right track." Howie looked around the stable to see if anyone else was listening. "Come closer," he whispered, "and I'll tell you my idea."

9

A Better Plan

"Howie's plan makes more sense than Eddie's," Melody said after Howie told them his idea. "Searching every stall won't be hard."

Howie nodded. "If we find that white horse munching oats, then we can prove it isn't a unicorn," he said.

"We'll also prove Liza's head is full of oatmeal," Eddie added.

"What if we don't find him?" Liza asked.

"Don't worry," Eddie said. "He's here."

"Let's go," Howie said. He swung open the stall door and led his friends to the end of the stable. The tiny puppy chased after his untied shoelace, but Howie ignored her.

Howie opened the first stall door and the four friends peeked inside. A horse the color of dirt swung its head around and looked at them with huge brown eyes. A man was busy braiding green and red ribbons into the horse's mane. He looked at the four kids.

"What do you want?" he asked.

Howie smiled. "Sorry, we were looking for someone else." Then he closed the door and led his friends to the next stall. They went from stall to stall. They were halfway down the long stable and, so far, all they saw were brown, black, and gray horses.

Howie, Liza, Eddie, and Melody hurried to the next stall. Before Howie had a chance to open the gate, a deep voice made his hand freeze on the latch.

"I don't want you snooping," Mr. Withers said. "It could be dangerous. What are you looking for?"

Liza faced the stable owner. "We were

just looking at the horses," she said with a shaky voice. "We didn't mean to bother anyone."

"Listen," Mr. Withers said. "Giving sleigh rides at the mall is the biggest moneymaking event for the stables. The horses need to look their best. Unless you plan to help, you'll need to play somewhere else."

"We'll help," Howie blurted before Mr. Withers walked away. "We'll do anything you want us to."

"Anything?" Mr. Withers said with a smile.

Melody, Liza, Howie, and Eddie nodded. They knew it was their only chance to search the rest of the stable.

Mr. Withers nodded. "It's a deal," he said. "Follow me."

Eddie took a deep breath. "I have a feeling I'm going to regret this."

10

Nothing but Muck

The four friends followed Mr. Withers to the storage room. They gulped when he handed them shovels.

Mr. Withers smiled. "You can start by mucking out the stalls," he said. Then he went outside to get the sleighs ready.

"What does 'muck' mean?" Eddie asked.

Liza took a deep breath. "I'll tell you," she said. "But I don't think you really want to know."

As soon as Eddie found out what they were supposed to do, he dropped the shovel on the floor. "No way," he said. "I'm not shoveling THAT!"

"You will," Howie told him, "if you want to prove that the white horse is only a horse and not a unicorn."

"Of course it's a horse," Eddie said.

Liza picked up Eddie's shovel and handed it to him. "Then prove it. Besides, cleaning out the stalls is just part of taking care of a horse."

"Like feeding a dog is part of having a dog," Howie said.

"Liza's right," Melody said. "You have to take care of animals, even the yucky stuff. Unless you're too much of a baby."

Eddie grabbed the shovel from Liza. "I'll do it," he snapped. "But I won't like it." Then he stomped to a stall and went to work.

Melody giggled as the rest of them headed for a stall to clean. "I wish I had a camera," she said. "No one is going to believe we got Eddie to do real work."

The four kids worked hard to clean out the stalls. They made sure to put clean straw down on the floor.

"You know," Melody said when they were resting, "this isn't as bad as it sounded."

Eddie pinched his nose. "It wouldn't be so bad if I had a clothespin for my nose."

"But we didn't find the white horse," Liza said with a smile.

"We didn't find anything," Eddie said. "Nothing but stinky muck. But these horses are sort of neat to be around."

"Maybe Mr. Withers would let us work here," Howie said. "He could pay us by letting us ride the horses."

"Let's ask," Melody suggested.

The four friends found Mr. Withers outside, hitching a spotted pony to a sleigh. They told him their idea.

"We could clean out that old barn where we found the puppy and kitten," Liza said.

"That old barn? It hasn't been used for years," Mr. Withers said.

Just then a gust of wind blew around the corner of the Bailey City Stables. Liza was sure she heard bells ringing.

And then Liza had an idea. An excellent, wonderful, perfect idea.

11

A Special
Christmas Present

"It is a good idea," Melody said.

"Bailey City really needs one," Howie added.

Eddie didn't say anything at first. He twitched his shoelace in front of Liza's new kitten. Jingle Bells' yellow eyes watched the string. Eddie, Howie, and Melody sat on the floor in Liza's family room. Liza had just told them her idea.

"Turning Mr. Withers' empty barn into an animal shelter would never work," Eddie finally said.

"Why not?" Liza asked.

"Because," Eddie said, "animal shelters cost money. Mr. Withers doesn't have very much. Neither do we."

"That's true," Melody said. "Mr. With-

ers said the sleigh rides are the only way the stable earns enough to stay open."

"He could never afford to take care of homeless animals, too," Howie said sadly.

"But what if the barn didn't belong to Mr. Withers?" Liza asked. "Then he wouldn't have to pay for the animal shelter."

"And what if it started snowing chocolate Santas?" Eddie laughed.

Melody patted Liza's arm. "Your idea is good," she said. "But Mr. Withers owns that barn and that's all there is to it."

"He does now," Liza said with a wink. "But what if he gave it to Bailey City as a Christmas present?"

"I don't think you can gift wrap a barn," Eddie said. "There isn't enough ribbon to make the bow."

"Very funny," Liza said. "Mr. Withers wouldn't have to wrap it."

"You're not making any sense," Melody

said. "Why would Mr. Withers give Bailey City a barn?"

"Because," Howie interrupted, "then he wouldn't have to take care of it anymore. . . ."

"And Bailey City could turn it into an animal shelter," Liza finished.

"Do you think he would do it?" Melody asked.

Liza grinned at her friends. "There's only one way to find out!"

12

Christmas Magic

The horses were hitched to their sleighs when Liza, Melody, Howie, and Eddie arrived at the Bailey City Stables on Christmas Eve. They were excited about the mayor's announcement.

A small group of people were clustered in front of the stable. The mayor cleared his throat and smiled.

"I have a special announcement to make," he finally said, and the crowd grew quiet. "Mr. Withers has made a generous donation of a barn to our city. The barn will be turned into the new Bailey City Animal Shelter."

Everybody looked at the stable owner. He blushed when the news camera pointed in his direction.

"Thanks to Mr. Withers' donation," the

mayor continued, "Bailey City will finally have an animal shelter that will be dedicated to keeping animals healthy and happy until good homes can be found for them."

The crowd cheered and clapped. "What made you think to donate the barn?" a news reporter asked.

"It — it wasn't my idea at all," Mr. Withers stammered and pointed at Liza, Melody, Howie, and Eddie. "It was theirs."

Cameras clicked and a television reporter stuck a microphone in front of Howie. "How did you come up with this idea?" the reporter asked.

Howie held up Lucky. "We found this puppy in the barn," he said. He made sure to speak slowly and clearly into the microphone.

"And I found a kitten there, too," Eddie bragged.

"They were both cold and hungry,"

Melody explained, smiling for the camera.

"There was no place to take them," Howie said. "So our parents let us keep them."

"Mr. Withers didn't know what to do with the empty barn, so Liza came up with the idea of turning it into an animal shelter," Melody said.

The camera pointed at Liza and the reporter stuck the microphone in front of her.

"Your idea has brought Christmas magic to all the animals of Bailey City," the reporter said as the crowd cheered and clapped.

"And that's exactly what it was," Liza said shyly. "Magic."

13

Unicorn Magic

"There's your unicorn," Melody giggled as Mr. Withers led a white horse and sleigh out of the stables. The horse's mane was decorated with red and green ribbons, and a giant red-and-white candy cane stuck out between its ears. Tiny bells jingled when the horse shook his head to knock off the rapidly falling snow. The cameras had been packed up and almost everyone had left after the mayor's announcement.

"That's not my unicorn," Liza said, stepping out of the way of the sleigh.

Howie patted Liza's shoulder. "I bet that's what you saw. After all, we never really proved there was a unicorn."

"We didn't see one, because there

wasn't one to see," Eddie said matter-of-factly.

"We'll never see one now," Liza said wistfully.

"What do you mean?" Melody asked. "Did you finally stop believing in unicorns?"

Liza shook her head quickly. "No. I just mean that the unicorn's work is done. It came here to get Mr. Withers to help weak animals, and now it'll go somewhere else. But it left some of its magic behind."

Eddie checked the bottoms of his shoes. "I hope I didn't step in any of its magic."

Liza giggled and wiped a snowflake off her nose. "I'm talking about the kind of magic inside us. We started the Bailey City Animal Shelter and we can keep the magic going by volunteering to work there."

"Let's do it," Melody and Howie agreed together.

Debbie Dadey and Marcia Thornton Jones have fun writing stories together. When they both worked at an elementary school in Lexington, Kentucky, Debbie was the school librarian and Marcia was a teacher. During their lunch break in the school cafeteria, they came up with the idea of the Bailey School kids.

Debbie and her family now live in Aurora, Illinois. Marcia and her husband still live in Kentucky where she continues to teach. How do these authors still write together? They talk on the phone and use computers and fax machines!

"What about you?" Liza asked Eddie.

Eddie rolled his eyes. "Will there be any of that stinky mucking to do?"

Liza laughed. "Maybe just a little."

"Oh, all right," Eddie said. "But I'm going to need lots of magic to help me."

Just then, a gentle breeze blew past the four friends and Eddie heard a jingle followed by a neigh. It came from the direction of the new Bailey City Animal Shelter.

Eddie looked through the swirling snow and, just for a second, he was sure he saw Mr. Withers standing next to a unicorn. But when he blinked and looked again, all he saw was the swirling snow.